Walt Disney's Pinocchio

Adapted by Nikki Grimes
Illustrated by Phil Ortiz
and Diana Wakeman

A GOLDEN BOOK • NEW YORK
Western Publishing Company, Inc., Racine, Wisconsin 53404

Once upon a time, a wood-carver named Geppetto carved a wonderful little puppet and named him Pinocchio.

"How I wish Pinocchio were a real boy," Geppetto said to himself. "He would be my very own son."

Geppetto did not know that a fairy had heard his wish. That very night, while he slept, the fairy brought the wooden puppet to life.

The Blue Fairy spoke to Pinocchio. "You're still a puppet," she said. "But if you are brave, truthful, and unselfish, you will become a real boy."

Pinocchio promised to try his best, with Jiminy Cricket to help him along the way.

When Geppetto woke to find that his puppet was alive, he danced for joy.

Like all boys, Pinocchio had to go to school that day. He hadn't gotten very far when he met a selfish man named Stromboli. Stromboli ran a puppet theater and promised to make Pinocchio a star.

Everyone loved the new puppet, the one
that danced without strings. Pinocchio loved
the bright lights and applause. He was indeed
a star.

When the show was over, Stromboli locked poor Pinocchio in a cage so he wouldn't escape. Pinocchio wept, but not even Jiminy Cricket could help him.

Just then, the Blue Fairy appeared.

"Pinocchio, why didn't you go to school today?" she asked.

"I—I was kidnapped by a green monster!" Pinocchio lied. At that moment, his nose began to tingle. Then it began to grow longer!

Pinocchio told more than one lie, but at last he told the truth.

"I will give you another chance," said the Blue Fairy. "But you must learn to do what is good and right."

With a wave of the fairy's wand, Pinocchio had his old nose back and the door of his cage opened.

Pinocchio headed straight for school, until
he met an evil coachman. The coachman
offered to take Pinocchio to Pleasure Island.

"Don't go, Pinoke!" pleaded Jiminy Cricket.
But Pinocchio jumped on a wagon drawn
by a sad-looking team of donkeys, and off
he rode.

Pleasure Island was a wondrous place. Fountains spouted lemonade. Big candy canes and lollipops grew like trees. A boy could do whatever he wanted because there were no grown-ups to stop him.

But soon Pinocchio realized that something terrible was happening to him on Pleasure Island. He was sprouting donkey ears—and a tail! Soon he would be nothing more than a donkey to pull the coachman's wagon.

To escape Pleasure Island, Pinocchio dived
off a cliff into the sea, with Jiminy Cricket
close behind. They swam all the way back to
the mainland and went to Geppetto's shop.

Geppetto was not home, but Pinocchio and Jiminy found a note.

The note said that Geppetto had gone searching for Pinocchio, but he'd ended up in the belly of Monstro the whale instead.

"This is all my fault!" cried Pinocchio. "I must find my father."

Pinocchio wasted no time. He returned to the shore and dived back into the ocean. At last he found Monstro the whale. When Monstro opened his huge mouth to swallow some fish, Pinocchio swam in, too.

"Oh, Pinocchio!" cried Geppetto. "Is it really you? But what is wrong with your ears?"

Pinocchio explained to Geppetto what had happened on Pleasure Island. Together they then tried to figure out how to escape. The answer was to build a fire.

The smoke from the fire made Monstro
sneeze. He sneezed so hard that Pinocchio
and Geppetto were thrown out of Monstro's
mouth and back into the sea.

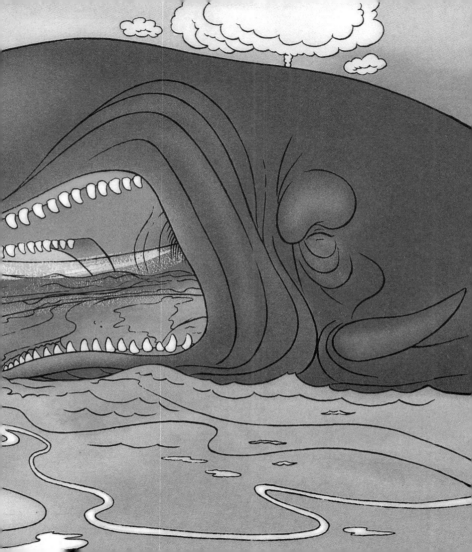

The long swim back to land was too
much for Geppetto. Brave little Pinocchio
fought the waves and helped his
father reach shore safely.

But Pinocchio was too exhausted to save himself. Geppetto finally found him lying facedown among the rocks.

Geppetto carried Pinocchio's lifeless body home and laid him down. Then he knelt beside Pinocchio and wept.

But soon a soft blue light slowly filled the room, and the Blue Fairy appeared once more.

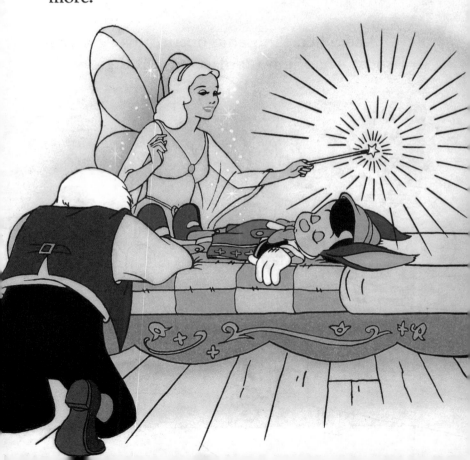

"Pinocchio, you have proven yourself brave, truthful, and unselfish," said the Blue Fairy gently. "Now you will become a real boy."

And when Pinocchio opened his eyes, that is just what he was at last—a real live boy.